Oscar's Best Friends

Look out for other
LITTLE DOLPHIN titles:

Hattie's New House
Party Time, Poppy!
Milo's Big Mistake

Oscar's Best Friends

LUCY DANIELS

Illustrated by DAVID MELLING

AN
APPLE
PAPERBACK

Scholastic Inc.
New York   Toronto   London   Auckland   Sydney
Mexico City   New Delhi   Hong Kong   Buenos Aires

LONG BEACH

SAMMY

N

LITTLE DOLPHIN

MILO

CAVES

STARFISH
ISLAND

TO SANDY
BAY

SEAWEED
FOREST

CORNELIUS

To Mackenzie Snowdon

Special thanks for Jan Burchett and Sara Vogler

ISBN 0-439-68199-5

12 11 10 9 8 7 6 5 4 3   8 9 10/0

Printed in the U.S.A.
First Scholastic printing, April 2005

CHAPTER ONE

"I had a wonderful vacation at Puffin Shore," said Little Dolphin, "but it's great to be back home!" He was rolling around in the warm waters of Urchin Bay with his dolphin friends Milo and Poppy.

"My mom and dad took me on a Whale Express tour," chirped Poppy. "We went through Cuttlefish Cove and around Pilchard Point —

and look what I got from Walrus
Lagoon." She did a twirl to show off
the pretty pebble neck-
lace she was
wearing.

"Where did you go for
your vacation, Milo?" she asked.
Milo thought hard. "I can't
remember the name," he said at
last. "But it was sunny and there
were lots of waves!"

Little Dolphin grinned. Milo was such a scatterbrain. "Oscar should be home from Sandy Bay soon," he said. "I heard it's really cool and trendy there."

"And he's bound to have lots of funny stories to tell," added Milo. "That octopus gets himself into a tangle wherever he goes!"

"I can't wait to see him!" whistled Poppy. She spun around with excitement, knocking Milo into a clump of seaweed.

"Let's play something—before Poppy spins herself into a tizzy!" Little Dolphin exclaimed as Milo struggled out from the floppy leaves.

"I got a new board game on my vacation. Wait here."

He darted off along the coral reef and into his cave, then swam back clutching the game under his flipper. "It's called Flotsam and Jetsam," he told them.

He showed his friends the board with its black-and-white square markings, along with a shell box of flat pebbles used to play the game. Half the pebbles were black and the others were white. "The board is made from a bit of the old wreck at Puffin Shore," he told them proudly. "Mom and I swam around it—

it's much bigger than our old wreck here at Urchin Bay."

Poppy peered eagerly at the box of pebbles and the squares on the board. "How do you play?" she asked.

Little Dolphin began to explain, "One side has the white pebbles and the other side has the black—" He stopped. Someone was swimming over to them.

It was Oscar!

"Hello, Oscar!" they all called. "Welcome back!"

They waited for Oscar to come up to them, waving all eight arms at once. He usually tangled himself into a big slippery knot!

But today Oscar just gave one tiny cool flick of an arm.

Little Dolphin wondered what was wrong with him. He didn't seem like his usual bouncy self.

"How was your vacation, Oscar?" asked Milo.

"Best ever,"
said Oscar
casually.

"What did
you do there?"
demanded Poppy,
spinning around him.

Oscar just shrugged.

Then Little Dolphin noticed they
were being watched. Two squids
were lounging on the sand
nearby. They looked really cool.
One was wearing a cap and the
other wore sunglasses. They waved
a couple of arms at Oscar.

"That's Smudge and Blot,"
Oscar explained proudly,

"my new friends from Sandy Bay."

Smudge and Blot glided over to them, squirting out hazy clouds of squid ink.

"Give me a high eight, my friend!" called Smudge. He and Oscar swam at each other and slapped all their eight arms together.

Then Smudge turned and looked at the dolphins. "Who are these guys, Osc?" he drawled.

Osc? thought Little Dolphin in surprise. He'd never heard Oscar called that before.

"They're the friends I told you about," Oscar drawled back. "Little Dolphin, Milo, and Poppy."

"Give me a high eight!" squeaked Milo, waving his flippers up and down at the squids.

"You've only got two flippers!" whispered Oscar, looking embarrassed.

"Oh, yes," clicked Milo, "I forgot...."

"So what do you all get up to, here in Urchin Bay?" asked Smudge.

"Yeah," added Blot, peering at them over his sunglasses. "What do you do for fun?"

Little Dolphin pushed his new game toward them. "I've got a new game," he chirped. "It's called Flotsam and Jetsam. You can join in, if you want."

"A board game?" said Smudge.

"Bor-ing!" said Blot.

Little Dolphin knew Oscar loved board games. But today he just looked away, as if he found them boring, too.

Feeling rather silly,

Little Dolphin nudged his new game under some seaweed.

"I know! We'll show you a dolphin tower!" said Poppy. "I'll be at the bottom." She stood on her tail on the seabed. Milo perched upright on her nose. Then Little Dolphin swam up and balanced on top of Milo's nose. "This is our best one yet!" whistled Poppy, trying not to wobble.

"Is that it?" asked Smudge. He didn't sound very impressed.

"No, I'm sure we can do more!" chirped Poppy. "How about a *spinning* dolphin tower?"

"Uh-oh—do you know anything about this, Little Dolphin?" Milo squeaked up to him, sounding alarmed.

"No, I don't!" Little Dolphin called back.

Then, without a word of warning, Poppy started to spin!

There was a flurry of flippers and swirling sand—and the dolphin tower collapsed in a heap on the seabed!

CHAPTER TWO

"We've never tried a spinning tower before," Little Dolphin squeaked, feeling embarrassed.

Blot shrugged, looking bored. "We've got to liven things up around here, Smudge, my friend," he said.

"Yeah!" agreed Smudge. "And I know just what we need." He flicked off his cap with one tentacle and pulled out a yo-yo made of two shiny black shells with the other. "The Riptide!" he announced.

Little Dolphin, Milo, and Poppy-gazed admiringly at it. They all had yo-yos, but theirs were nothing like this.

"It's the best in the ocean," Oscar told them as the yo-yo flashed around their heads. "It's even got reflector shells!"

Smudge made the Riptide whip out to the side and back, quick as a flash. "No one else can do that trick," he boasted. "I call it the Supercrab.

And now for my Electric Eel..."
The yo-yo wiggled through the
water, flashing as it went.

"It's so *deep!*" drawled Blot.
Little Dolphin wondered
what Blot meant. "It's not deep
here," he explained. "The water's
very shallow near the reef. If you
want deep water, you have to go
to..." He stopped. Smudge and
Blot were laughing at him!

"You don't understand, Little
Dolphin," whispered Oscar

hurriedly. "*Deep* means 'great' or 'cool'. It's trendy talk in Sandy Bay."

Little Dolphin felt *very* silly now. He almost wished a giant clam would come and swallow him up.

Smudge flicked the yo-yo neatly back into his cap. "Don't suppose any of you guys can handle the Riptide?" he dared them.

"I'd like a try!" exclaimed Milo. "It's such a great...I mean *deep* yo-yo."

Smudge tossed the Riptide to Milo and flopped casually onto a rock to watch. Blot and Oscar draped themselves next to him.

Hooking the Riptide's string
over his flipper, Milo gave it a
spin. But it was much too fast
for him! It whizzed out, flashing
as it spun, then sped back
and bumped him
hard on the nose!
Smudge and
Blot swayed with
laughter.
Poor Milo!
Little Dolphin and
Poppy rushed over
to him..
"I'm OK," he
insisted, blinking hard. "It
doesn't hurt."

Little Dolphin could see that his friend's nose was very red. But he guessed Milo wouldn't admit it was sore in front of the squids.

Poppy picked some seaweed and put it on her head. "Hey, I have a *deep* cap, too!" she announced. "Just like Smudge." She and Milo plonked themselves down next to the squids.

Little Dolphin didn't want to be left out, so he swam over and perched next to Milo. But he soon found that lounging on a rock isn't easy when you don't have arms.

Just then, Vinnie the shark
swam by. Little Dolphin saw his
mouth drop open with surprise as
he looked at the three wobbling
dolphins.

"Hi, Vinnie!" drawled Milo.
"Meet the new guys from Sandy
Bay." He tried to wave a casual
flipper and fell off the rock onto
his nose. Now it looked redder
than ever!

Vinnie grinned,
showing all his
teeth.

"Want to be cool, do you?" he said smoothly. "I've got just the thing back at my cave. Fin stickers with CHILL OUT! written on them. They're a bargain. They'll only cost you—"

"Vinnie!" came a sharp voice behind him. "I want a word with you."

"Oh, no! It's that Hattie again!" Vinnie gulped. "I'm off!" With one flick of his tail, he disappeared around the reef.

Hattie the hermit crab arrived, riding on an upturned bucket, which was strapped to the back of Fergal the turtle. "Did you see where that pesky shark went?" demanded Hattie. Her whiskers quivered crossly. "He's been selling things nobody needs—as usual. He just sold Fergal this bucket and told him it's a shell protector. I'm going to get him a refund!"

"Shell protector!" scoffed Blot, looking at Fergal over his sunglasses.

"Silly turtle!" added Smudge. He nudged Oscar, who gave an embarrassed grin.

Poor Fergal turned bright pink and disappeared into his shell.

Hattie glared at Oscar and the two squids. Then she stared hard at Little Dolphin, Milo, and Poppy. "What's the matter with you guys, wobbling on that rock like jellyfish?" she demanded. "You look really stupid. Come on, Fergal. Let's find Vinnie!" She tapped Fergal's bucket and Fergal swam away as fast as he could, with Hattie clinging on tightly.

Little Dolphin looked at Poppy and Milo. Maybe Hattie was right. They must all look very silly flapping their flippers as they tried to balance on the rock. But Little Dolphin wasn't going to say anything — he wanted to be cool and deep, like Oscar and his friends.

"I've got an idea," drawled Smudge as he slid smoothly down to the seabed. "Let's play Roughball."

"Deep!" said Blot.

"Yeah," copied Oscar. "Deep!"

Little Dolphin whistled in alarm. "No! We're not allowed!" Only older sea creatures played that game, because it could be dangerous. Milo's big brother, Frank, played for the Urchin Bay Slammers, but he was almost grown up.

"Not allowed?" scoffed Smudge. "Who says so?"

"All our moms," Little Dolphin said. "None of us are allowed to play."

Poppy and Milo nodded. Oscar didn't say anything, but Little Dolphin knew his mom wouldn't let him play, either.

Smudge and Blot rolled their eyes at each other.

Little Dolphin decided he didn't care now if Smudge and Blot made fun of them. Roughball was dangerous and he didn't want anyone to get hurt.

"No point hanging around with a bunch of scaredy shrimps, Blot, my friend," said Smudge.

"Too true!" agreed Blot.

"But I'll see you tomorrow, guys, won't I?" called Oscar anxiously as they turned to go.

"Sure," said Smudge. "See you tomorrow, Osc."

And the two squids swam away in a cloud of ink.

CHAPTER THREE

"Smudge and Blot are so *deep*," said Oscar as they watched the squids swim out of sight.

"Do you think they were joking about playing Roughball?" Little Dolphin clicked anxiously.

"Don't worry, Little Dolphin," chirped Milo. "We'll think of a different game that we can all play tomorrow."

"Let's play Sea Monsters!" squealed Poppy, spinning up and down. "We can meet at the old wreck tomorrow morning."

"Oh, yes!" agreed Oscar. "Sea-Monsters is great!" Then he let his arms flop. "I mean *deep*," he said awkwardly. "I'll ask Smudge and Blot to come along!"

But when Oscar arrived at the old wrecked ship the next morning, he was on his own. There was no sign of Smudge and Blot.

"We can start the game now that you're here, Oscar," Little Dolphin chirped brightly.

"I'll be the Monster of the Wreck."
He scooped up some long shells
with his mouth so that they stuck
out like big teeth.

"I'll be the Dreaded
Flabberflop!" squeaked Poppy,
draping seaweed all over
herself and waving her flippers
menacingly.

"I'll be the Sand Serpent, then," chirped Milo. "I'll bury myself in the seabed and you have to find me—unless I find you first!"

"Try not to get sand in your ears this time!" Poppy grinned.

Little Dolphin turned to Oscar. "Who are you going to be?" he asked.

But Oscar wasn't listening. He was looking at a yellow coral bush on the other side of the wreck. Little Dolphin peered at the bush.

Smudge and Blot were there, making ink rings in the water.

Smudge beckoned
to Oscar with
one of his long
tentacles.

"See you later,"
said Oscar,
sounding pleased.
And he swam off
to join them.

The Sea Monsters watched as
Smudge began juggling with some
conch shells.

"I thought Oscar had agreed
to play with *us*," exclaimed Milo,
sounding annoyed.

"We're just not *deep* enough,"
said Poppy sadly.

"Never mind, we can still play with three!" chirped Little Dolphin. "Go ahead, Milo."

Milo disappeared to hide.

Looking very fierce with his big monster teeth, Little Dolphin edged around the wreck.

Poppy the Dreaded Flabberflop followed. They glided silently along, nosing at the sand for signs of Milo the Sand Serpent. Where was he? Then they heard sounds from the other side of the wreck. They darted over.

"Got you, Milo!" whistled Poppy.

But it wasn't Milo. It was Smudge and Blot, and they were teaching Oscar a new juggling game with brightly colored pebbles. It looked like fun. They were so busy they didn't notice Little Dolphin and Poppy watching them.

"I wish I had arms to juggle with." Poppy sighed.

Milo's head popped up from the sand nearby. "Why have you stopped looking for me?" he spluttered, forgetting to be the Sand Serpent.

Then he saw Smudge, Blot, and Oscar, who were now all making clever ink shapes in the water.

"Why can't they play games
we dolphins can join in with?"
he grumbled.

Little Dolphin spat out his
monster teeth. "Let's go!" he
clicked. "Sea Monsters doesn't
seem so much fun anymore."

Poppy shook off her Flabberflop

seaweed, and the three friends
swam away from the wreck,
leaving Oscar, Smudge, and Blot
doing high eights with one another.

Milo swished his tail angrily.
"I wish Oscar had never made
friends with those squids!" he
clicked. "I don't think I'll ever
speak to him again!"

CHAPTER FOUR

"What should we play today?"
asked Little Dolphin as he bobbed
in the waves with Poppy and Milo
the next morning.

"What about No Escape?"
suggested Milo. "There's an
empty cave by the clam beds.
It'll make a perfect prison."

No Escape was one of their
favorite games.

"But we need Oscar to be the Catcher for that," Little Dolphin reminded him. When Oscar was the Catcher, he used all his eight arms to block them and they had great fun trying to wriggle past him without being caught. They didn't escape very often!

"Oscar won't play," said Poppy sadly. "He just hangs around with Smudge and Blot, juggling or doing high eights or lounging on rocks—things dolphins can't do!"

"We *can* play without Oscar," said Milo firmly. "*I'll* be the Catcher."

"But how are you going
to keep us prisoner?" asked
Poppy. "You don't have any arms
to catch us with."

"Flippers are just as good!"
insisted Milo.

So they swam over the clam
beds to the cave, and Little
Dolphin and Poppy darted
inside, to get ready to escape.

Then Milo tried to block the entrance. "You're my prisoners," he whistled fiercely. "There is no escape!"

Little Dolphin made a dart for the cave opening. Milo dived forward to stop him—and left a big gap for Poppy to dash through! Milo spotted her and whirled around—so Little Dolphin saw his chance, and he escaped, too!

Poor Milo. Whatever he did, Little Dolphin and Poppy kept escaping. And when Poppy spun toward him at top speed, he squealed and scurried off to try and hide with the clams!

"The Catcher's not supposed to be scared!" clicked Poppy as she swam back into the cave.

"But I thought you were going to drill a hole in my belly!" complained Milo.

Little Dolphin slumped to the floor. "We're not having much fun, are we?" he said. The game wasn't the same without Oscar. A Catcher needed plenty of long arms.

"It's all Oscar's fault," grumbled Milo. "He brought those two squids to Urchin Bay."

Sadly, they set off for home, back over

the clam beds and around the
seaweed bushes. They steered
clear of Ragged Rocks, a place
with nasty, sharp rocks that
towered up from the seabed.

But as they passed, Little
Dolphin saw someone playing
in there. "Look!" he clicked.

Poppy and Milo stopped to
look, too.

"It's Smudge and Blot,"
clicked Poppy. "And
Oscar!"

Little Dolphin whistled
in horror. "They're
playing Roughball!"

"But Oscar's too young!" whistled Milo. "My brother Frank's always coming home bandaged when he plays, and he's much older."

They watched anxiously. Smudge and Blot were on one team and Oscar was on the other.

Oscar didn't seem to be enjoying himself much. He was gripping the heavy ball tightly in one arm and swimming nervously toward his goal—a hole in one of the big jagged rocks.

Smudge suddenly leaped on him, tugging him down to the seabed. Then Blot barged in, shoved Oscar aside, and grabbed the ball with one of his long tentacles.

"Leave Oscar alone!" whistled Poppy. "That must be against the rules!"

"No, it's not," Milo told her. "It's a rough game."

Oscar picked himself up and chased after Smudge and Blot. The two squids had nearly reached their goal, tossing the ball from arm to arm. But as Smudge whacked the ball

toward the goal with a tentacle,
Oscar darted forward and pushed
the ball away. It was a great
save!

"Hurray!" whistled Poppy,
spinning with excitement.

"Good job, Oscar!" called
Milo. Then he grinned. "Oops,
I forgot I'm not talking to him!"

But the ball had smashed
against the rock and loosened a
big jagged boulder. It wobbled
dangerously!

Little Dolphin could see that
Oscar was right underneath and
the boulder was going to fall.
"Look out, Oscar!" he whistled
in alarm.

It was too late. The boulder
tumbled down with a terrible
crash and hit Oscar!

CHAPTER FIVE

Little Dolphin rushed over to Oscar. Milo and Poppy followed close behind.

Oscar was lying on the seabed. There was a nasty cut on one of his arms. "Ow! It hurts!" he groaned.

"Poor Oscar!" squeaked Poppy. "You're bleeding!"

Smudge and Blot took one look and began to back away.

"That's bad, Blot," said Smudge anxiously.

"Yeah," replied Blot. "What are we going to do, Smudge?"

"Dunno," said Smudge. "The sight of blood makes me go all funny."

The two squids clung to each other and quivered.

Oscar turned to Little Dolphin, Poppy, and Milo. "Can you help me to get home?"

he pleaded. "I don't think I can swim."

Little Dolphin dabbed Oscar's wound with a piece of sponge. "Don't worry, Oscar," he clicked. "We'll get you home."

"But how?" squeaked Poppy.

"Oscar will be here forever!" quavered Blot, tangling his arms into an anxious knot.

"He'll bleed to death!" whimpered Smudge, covering his eyes.

Little Dolphin ignored the silly squids and thought hard. "I've got it!" he whistled. "Milo and I will tow Oscar home. He can hold on to our fins. It'll be all right if we swim really slowly. Poppy, you go tell Oscar's mom we're on our way."

Poppy nodded, then sped off.

Oscar wrapped an arm around each of his friends' fins and held on tightly. "I'm ready," he said bravely.

Then Little Dolphin and Milo slowly towed Oscar away from

Ragged Rocks and toward his cave.

The next day, Little Dolphin, Milo, and Poppy went to visit their injured friend.

"My arm's much better now," Oscar told them. "Thank you for helping me home. I haven't seen Smudge and Blot at all."

"Maybe they feel a little embarrassed," Little Dolphin said. "They weren't much help yesterday."

"Never mind, Oscar," chirped Milo. "Come for a swim with us instead!"

Little Dolphin grinned. He was glad Milo had forgotten that he was never going to speak to Oscar again.

"Great!" said Oscar, with a big smile.

They all swam along the reef, darting in and out of the coral and chasing one another until they were dizzy. But then they heard a familiar voice.

"Osc, my friend!" It was Smudge. He was gliding over the seabed toward them—and Blot was right behind. The two squids looked very awkward.

"Sorry about yesterday, Osc," muttered Smudge. "Hope your arm's OK now."

"It's much better!" said Oscar. "Thanks to my friends here, I'm fine."

"Yeah," said Smudge shyly. "We weren't very good friends to you yesterday. We got you to play Roughball..."

"...and we didn't help when you got hurt," finished Blot.

"We just came to say sorry..." said Smudge, twiddling his cap, "...to everybody."

"And we wanted to ask something," added Blot in a very small voice. "Could we play with you guys?"

Oscar looked at Little Dolphin, Milo, and Poppy.

They all beamed. "Of course!" they replied.

Oscar waved his arms happily—and got himself into a terrible knot.

Everyone cheered and dived in to untie him, even Smudge and Blot.

They were still in a wriggling heap on the seabed when Hattie and Fergal came by.

"You all seem to be having fun again!" Hattie laughed. "That's a relief!"

"Where's your bucket...I mean your shell protector, Fergal?" asked Poppy.

"Hattie got me a refund," said

Fergal shyly, looking at Smudge
and Blot.

"We shouldn't
have laughed
at you, Fergal,
my man," said
Smudge.

"Don't worry," Fergal smiled,
going pink. "I did look silly!"

"Well, now that we're all here
together, what should we play?"
asked Poppy happily.

Smudge turned to Little
Dolphin. "Could I try having a
ride on your back?" he asked.
"Like Osc did when you towed
him home?"

"Yeah," agreed Blot. "It looked like a really cool way to travel!"

"Hop on, then, Smudge," Little Dolphin chirped.

"And I'll take you, Blot," added Milo.

"Deep!" Blot cheered.

"I'm not being left out," snorted Hattie, waving her claws. "Come here, Poppy." And she scrambled onto Poppy's back and clung on tightly.

Oscar and Fergal waved as Little Dolphin, Milo, and Poppy swam around them.

Little Dolphin swam so fast that Smudge's cap whizzed off. "Don't stop!" called Smudge. "I'll get it later."

"This is *dee-ee-eep*!" called Blot as Milo leaped out of the water.

"I'm glad we're all playing together!" whistled Poppy. She began to spin with happiness.

"You're making me dizzy!" Hattie laughed, her claws waving wildly.

At last, the rides came to an end.

"What should we play now?" asked Blot eagerly.

"Let's teach Smudge and Blot No Escape!" squealed Poppy.

"As long as I'm not the Catcher!" chirped Milo.

"Don't worry, Milo," said Oscar. "I'll be the Catcher." He smiled at Little Dolphin. "But first, I think we should play Flotsam and Jetsam!"

"*Deep!*" agreed Smudge and Blot.

And everyone cheered.